THE
McELDERRY
BOOK
OF
GREEK
MYTHS

The McElderry Book of Grimms' Fairy Tales

The McElderry Book of Aesop's Fables

THE McELDERRY BOOK OF GREEK MYTHS

Retold by Eric A. Kimmel

Illustrated by Pep Montserrat

MARGARET K. McELDERRY BOOKS
New York   London   Toronto   Sydney

To Renée Rothauge, Warrior Princess—E. A. K.

To the people I love, who in a way are in this book.
Thanks to all of them, especially Gabo, who enjoyed and
suffered the process with me in such a warm and close
way.—P. M.

MARGARET K. McELDERRY BOOKS

An imprint of Simon & Schuster Children's Publishing Division

1230 Avenue of the Americas, New York, New York 10020

Text copyright © 2008 by Eric A. Kimmel

Illustrations copyright © 2008 by Pep Montserrat

All rights reserved, including the right of reproduction in whole or in part in any form.

Book design by Debra Sfetsios and Michael McCartney

The text for this book is set in KurosawaHand.

The illustrations for this book are rendered electronically.

Manufactured in China

10

Library of Congress Cataloging-in-Publication Data

Kimmel, Eric A.

The McElderry book of Greek myths / Eric A. Kimmel ; illustrated by Pep Montserrat.

p. cm.

ISBN-13: 978-1-4169-1534-8

ISBN-10: 1-4169-1534-6 (hardcover)

1. Mythology, Greek—Juvenile literature. I. Montserrat, Pep. II. Title.

BL783.K56 2008

398.20938—dc22

2005031010

0914 SCP

CONTENTS

Why Greek myths?

Why bother retelling these ancient stories? Most of them date back to the Bronze Age, centuries before recorded history began. What can they possibly have to say to children who live in a world of cell phones, the Internet, iPods, and DVDs?

More than most people realize.

First of all, they are wonderful stories. Parents shared them with children for generations before they were written down. The hero who goes on a dangerous quest; the heroine who strives for more than her culture will allow; and the person who attempts too much and fails, but still remains a hero, are basic themes in the movies we see and the books we read today.

Second, the myths are the foundation of our language and literature. References to the myths can be found throughout Shakespeare's plays. They are part of our everyday language. When we hear someone say that they are opening a "Pandora's Box" or making a "Promethean" effort to find the "Golden Fleece," they are referring to the myths.

Third, the myths stretch our imagination. They inspire us to strive for things we can only dream about. There is a clear connection between Icarus's wings and Neil Armstrong's walk on the moon.

The myths contain the hopes and dreams of humanity. Make them your own.

PROMETHEUS

PROMETHEUS AND HIS BROTHER, Epimetheus, were Titans, members of a race of giants. At the beginning of time the gods fought a great battle with the Titans to decide who would rule the universe. The gods won. Most of the Titans were destroyed.

The gods created the earth from the bodies of dead Titans. Their bones became rocks and mountains. Their blood became the sea, lakes, and rivers. Their eyes became the stars, and their hair, the grass and trees. Prometheus and his brother had fought alongside the gods. As a reward they were given the task of filling the earth with living creatures.

Living forms already crawled on the earth. They were pale, shapeless creatures. Zeus, the ruler of the gods, asked Epimetheus to give each of these creatures a gift. Prometheus was to inspect his work and make sure that every creature had received something.

Epimetheus eagerly handed out the gifts of the gods. To some he gave the gift of flying through the air. Others received the gift of swimming in the ocean. Some received sharp teeth and claws. Others received the ability to run fast, to dig deep, and to jump high. Some received feathers and fur. Others received scales and shells. The lion's mane, the zebra's stripes, the elephant's trunk,

the peacock's tail, and the leopard's spots were all received from Epimetheus.

At last all of the gifts had been handed out. Epimetheus called for Prometheus to come and look over what he had done.

"This is good work," Prometheus said. Then he noticed two weak, naked creatures crawling on the ground. "What about these? These are human beings. Don't you have a gift for them?"

"I never noticed the humans. I forgot all about them," Epimetheus stammered. "What can we do? I've given all of Zeus's gifts to the other animals. There is nothing left."

"We must find something for them," Prometheus said. "Otherwise, they will be the lowest, most miserable creatures on earth. Since you have nothing left down here, I'll go up to Mount Olympus, where the gods live. I'll see what I can find there."

Prometheus climbed to the top of Mount Olympus. He carried an unlit torch with him, for he knew exactly which gift he hoped to bring back. When no one was looking, he lit the torch on the wheel of the sun chariot that Apollo, the god of the sun, drove across the sky each day.

Prometheus hurried down the mountain. He presented the burning torch to the humans. "You will always be weak and naked," he said. "You will never possess the elephant's strength, the horse's speed, the snake's cunning, or the eagle's majesty. But with this gift you can become their master. This is fire. Use it wisely, and you can rule the earth. Use it unwisely, and you will destroy yourselves. The choice is yours."

The humans took the gift of fire from Prometheus. At first they used it to keep warm.

Later they learned to make clothes and tools. They learned to hunt and grow fruits and vegetables. Villages arose, then towns and cities.

Humans became masters of the earth. They ruled over the other animals, as they do to this day. Have they proved worthy of Prometheus's gift? Not always. Yet humans still have the power to choose.

Zeus became enraged when he learned what Prometheus had done. He never intended to give any earthly creature the gift of fire. With fire, humans could become wise and powerful. Someday they might even challenge the gods.

Zeus decreed a terrible punishment for Prometheus. He chained him to a rock at the top of a high mountain, where he remains today. There a hungry vulture tears at his flesh, which grows back as soon as it is swallowed. The torture is unending.

Sometimes, when Prometheus can endure no more, he groans and pulls against his chains, making the earth tremble. That is why we have earthquakes.

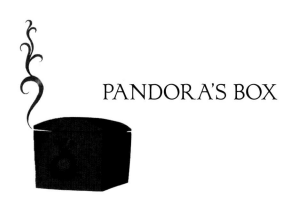

PANDORA'S BOX

EPIMETHEUS WEPT FOR HIS BROTHER Prometheus. He pleaded with Zeus to have mercy. "Those who steal from the gods must be punished," Zeus said. "Forget your brother. You cannot help him. His fate is sealed until the end of time."

"What about me?" Epimetheus asked. "Every animal has a companion. Wolves run in packs. Fish swim in schools. Birds fly in flocks. Zebras run in herds. Even lowly snails and slugs have mates. I have no one! Prometheus was more than a brother. He was my dearest friend. Without him I am truly alone."

Zeus pitied Epimetheus, so he created a woman to be his companion. All the gods gave her gifts.

Artemis gave her strength and courage.

Athena gave her wisdom.

Hera gave her majesty and grace.

Hermes gave her wit and cleverness.

Aphrodite gave her beauty.

Apollo gave her music and song.

The gods called the woman *Pandora,* which means "all gifts." It was a fitting name, for she had all the gifts that the gods could give.

Zeus carried Pandora to earth and presented her to Epimetheus. The Titan wept with joy when he saw his new bride. Pandora, too, was pleased. Her bridegroom was handsome, kind, and truly in love with her.

Pandora and Epimetheus were married. All the gods came down from Olympus to celebrate their wedding. Epimetheus thanked the gods for giving him Pandora. She had brought laughter and joy to his home.

Epimetheus took Pandora through his house. He showed her every room. He opened every chest and cupboard so that she could see what was inside.

"This house is now our home," Epimetheus said. "Everything here is yours as well as mine." However, Pandora noticed that there was one box he did not open.

"What about this one? What is in here?" she asked.

"Nothing you need to know about," Epimetheus said. "Leave that box alone. There is nothing inside that concerns you."

Epimetheus made Pandora promise never to open the box. She agreed, although she could not understand why. She couldn't help thinking, *What is inside that box? What secret does it contain that Epimetheus doesn't want me to see?*

Despite her curiosity, Pandora kept her promise. She never touched the box. She avoided going near it. She seldom looked at it.

Yet try as she might, she could not stop her curiosity from growing. *What is in that box?* she wondered.

One day while Epimetheus was out in the world, Pandora took a broom and began sweeping the house. She swept the dust from every room, until she came to the one where the box stood in the corner.

Pandora swept around it carefully, making sure not to touch it. She swept the dust into a dustpan. She was about to carry it away when she heard a voice calling her name.

"Pandora! Pandora! Let me out!"

It was a tiny voice, like the cry of a baby kitten. Pandora looked around the room. Who was calling her? She heard it again.

"Pandora! Pandora!"

It came from the box in the corner.

Pandora put down her broom. "Who are you?" she asked.

"A poor, helpless creature. I am shut up in this box with all my brothers and sisters. They are too weak to talk. We have been here for so long, without food or water. We have neither light nor air. Let us out! We will die if we remain here."

Pandora had promised Epimetheus that she would leave the box alone. However,

the gods had given her the gifts of kindness and compassion. She could not turn
away from a creature in trouble.

Pandora thought, *I know I promised not
to open the box. What if I just lift the lid a bit?
That would not really be opening it. I only want
to take a peek. If I see something nasty inside, I'll
shut it right away.*

Pandora got down on her knees before
the box. She lifted the lid just a crack,
and peeked in.

The lid flew off. A swarm
of creatures burst out of the box.
They surrounded Pandora, biting
and stinging until she bled. Then
they flew away.

Epimetheus came home. He found Pandora lying on the floor, bruised and swollen. Her eyes were red from weeping. The overturned box lay in the corner. He knew at once what had happened.

"I am so sorry," Pandora said. "I broke my promise. Something called to me from inside the box. I wanted to see what it was. I only meant to take a peek. Instead I ruined everything."

"Don't be sorry," said Epimetheus, taking her hand. "You made a mistake. That is all. The fault was mine. I should have explained what was in the box and why it had to remain closed.

"When I gave gifts to the animals, I had some ugly things left over that I thought no one deserved to have. Their names were Sorrow, Disease, Misery, Despair, and a host of other worries and misfortunes. I could not get rid of them, so I put them in the box. As long as they stayed inside, they could not trouble the world.

"I knew I could not keep them in the box

forever. One day they would get loose. That day has come, and there is nothing we can do about it. The gods created these troubles for a reason. They are part of creation, for better or for worse, and we must endure them."

At that moment Pandora heard another voice calling. "Pandora! Don't forget me! I am still here." It came from inside the box.

"Oh, no! Another misfortune!" Epimetheus groaned. "Perhaps we can hold on to this one."

He and Pandora looked in the box together. At the bottom they saw a shining creature with gold wings. It looked up at them and smiled.

"My name is Hope," the creature said. "You do not have to keep me in a box. Put me in your hearts and I will stay with you forever. As long as you have Hope, you need not fear misery or misfortune. With Hope you can overcome sorrow and despair. Nothing can defeat you, as long as you have Hope."

Pandora and Epimetheus lifted Hope from the box. They made a special place for her in their hearts, where she remained for the rest of their lives.

Hope is still with us. There is a special place for her in all our hearts. As long as she is there, the sorrows and troubles of the world can never defeat us.

PERSEPHONE AND HADES

AFTER DEFEATING THE TITANS, the gods divided the universe among themselves. Zeus became ruler of the heavens and the earth. His brother Poseidon claimed the oceans. His second brother, Hades, received the Underworld, the endless underground caverns that were the realm of the dead.

The underground kingdom was a gloomy place. At times it grew too stifling for Hades. He longed to breathe fresh air and feel the warm sun on his skin. Whenever he felt this way, he would hitch four black horses to his chariot and ride through a cave beneath Mount Etna that led to the world above.

Here Hades found his special place, a quiet valley where he enjoyed lying on the grass and picking flowers. Hades thought no one else knew about the valley. He was wrong. Aphrodite, the goddess of love, and her son, Eros, came here too.

One spring day as they rested beneath the trees, Eros said to his mother, "Why did you allow Zeus and his brothers to divide the universe? Why didn't you demand a realm for yourself?"

Aphrodite answered with a smile. "Why should I settle for a kingdom when all of creation is mine? The gods rule the universe, but I rule the gods."

"What do you mean?" Eros asked.

"What god or human can resist the power of love?" said Aphrodite. "When they fall in love, I become their master."

"That's true for most," said Eros. "However, I know someone who is immune to your power."

"Who is that?" Aphrodite asked.

"That dark fellow there!" said Eros. He pointed to Hades, who was driving his chariot through the hidden valley.

"You think so?" Aphrodite answered. "Give me your bow and one of your arrows. I will prove you wrong." Eros's arrows had a special power. Anyone they struck fell in love immediately.

Aphrodite fitted the arrow to the bowstring. She took careful aim. The arrow flew straight to its mark, striking deep into the heart of Hades.

Hades clutched his chest. *What is this?* he asked himself. *Something strange is happening.* He drove across the meadow, sighing like a young man in love.

"*I love trees! I love flowers! I love sunshine!*" Hades sang to himself. "*And most of all . . .*"

Across the meadow he saw a young woman gathering flowers. Her name was Persephone. She was the daughter of Demeter, who ruled over crops, plants, and all growing things.

"I love you!" Hades cried. He turned his horses and galloped

toward her, blowing kisses and shouting, "Beautiful maiden, how I adore you! Marry me! Be mine forever!"

Persephone let out a shriek. The ruler of the Underworld was frightening enough. Seeing him in love was absolutely terrifying. Persephone clutched her basket and ran.

Hades pursued her. "Let me look at your beautiful face! Do not run away!"

"Mother, help me!" Persephone screamed. Hades caught her around the waist as his chariot swept by. The ground split in two. Hades drove his horses through the opening. The ground closed, leaving nothing behind but an empty basket and bunches of wild-flowers scattered upon the grass.

Demeter went mad with grief when Persephone failed to return from the meadow. She searched the world by day and by night, seeking her missing daughter. The sun, the moon, and the stars helped her. Not a trace of Persephone could they find.

Demeter continued searching. She traveled on until she came to the island of Sicily. There she found a long, linen sash tangled in a thornbush. Demeter recognized it as one she had woven for Persephone.

"My daughter has been here!" Demeter cried. She called on the birds and insects to help her search. They explored every pebble, every blade of grass, until they found Persephone's basket and a trail of wildflowers leading from it.

The flowers led Demeter to the riverbank, where she discovered the tracks of chariot wheels leading to a crack in the earth.

"Hades has kidnapped Persephone!" Demeter cried. "I will go to Zeus. He must command Hades to set her free!"

Demeter hurried to Mount Olympus. She demanded that Zeus order Hades to release her daughter.

"I cannot," Zeus said. "Hades is my brother, not my subject. I cannot make him do anything."

"Hear me, Zeus!" Demeter said. "If Persephone is not returned, I will curse the earth. No rain will fall. Crops will shrivel in the fields. The world will become a lifeless wasteland if Persephone does not come back to me."

"I will try to help you," Zeus promised. He spoke to Hermes, the messenger of the gods. "Go

with Demeter to Hades. Try to persuade my brother to do what is right."

Hermes guided Demeter through the gates of the Underworld. They crossed the River Styx and journeyed through endless caverns until they came before the Lord of the Dead.

Hades sat on his throne. Persephone sat beside him, wearing a golden crown. Demeter threw her arms wide and shouted, "Persephone, my daughter! I have come to free you from this realm of shadows."

"Mother! I am so glad to see you," Persephone exclaimed. Something about her disturbed Demeter. She expected Persephone to look frightened. Instead her daughter seemed . . . happy!

"Demeter, Hermes, welcome to my kingdom," said Hades. "I hope you can stay with us awhile."

"I came to take back my daughter. I will not stay here one moment longer than I have to," Demeter snapped.

"But I don't want to leave," said Persephone. "Hades was wrong to carry me off. He is sorry and I have forgiven him. He could not help himself. Aphrodite had struck him with an arrow and so he fell in love. I believe she had an arrow for me, for I have fallen in love too. Hades is good and kind, Mother. He tries hard to please me. And there is so much to see and learn in this world below ground. The spirits of the dead no longer frighten me. They need comfort, which I can give them. I have important work down here. I want to stay."

"You cannot stay!" said Demeter. "Give back Hades' crown. You are coming with me."

"Persephone may be your daughter, but she is now my wife," Hades said. "You cannot take her from me if she does not wish to go."

Hermes stepped in to settle the matter. Turning to Hades, he said, "You took Persephone without her mother's consent. According to the laws of the world above, this marriage is not valid." He turned to Demeter. "According to the laws of the world below, no soul, living or dead, may leave this place if it has eaten anything, even if it were as small as a pomegranate seed." He looked at Persephone. "Have you eaten anything since Hades brought you here?"

"Only six pomegranate seeds," Persephone answered. "I was hungry."

"Then she must remain with me!" crowed Hades.

"I will destroy the world if she does!" Demeter threatened.

"Help me, Hermes!" Persephone pleaded. "How can I satisfy my husband and my mother?"

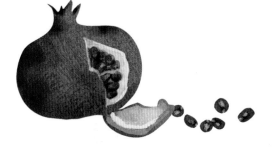

"I know a way," said Hermes. "Because you ate six pomegranate seeds, you must remain in the Underworld for six months of the year. For the other six months you must return to the world above to be with your mother."

"Thank you, Hermes," said Persephone. "How lucky I am! I have my mother and my husband. I have the world above and the world below. Let us celebrate, for you have made us all so happy."

Perhaps, but not quite. For six months of the year, when Persephone leaves the Underworld, Demeter's joy overflows. She blesses the earth. Crops ripen in the fields. Trees bring forth fruit. Warmth and light fill the world in this time of plenty. We call these seasons spring and summer.

When spring and summer pass, Persephone must return to the Underworld to be with her husband, Hades. The world turns cold and barren. Icy winds bring frost and snow. People huddle around fires to keep warm. But they do not lose hope. They know that spring will come again, and that Persephone will always return.

ECHO AND NARCISSUS

ECHO WAS A FOREST NYMPH, beautiful and kind. Artemis, goddess of the moon, loved her dearly. When Artemis came to the forest to hunt, she called on Echo to join her.

Echo, however, had one fault. She loved to talk. She chattered without stopping. It did not bother her one bit that nobody listened to anything she said.

Hera, the queen of the gods, once came to visit Artemis. Echo kept interrupting the two as they spoke. Artemis warned Echo to be silent, but she paid no attention. She prattled on and on until Hera lost patience. She turned to Echo and said, "You love to talk, and so you shall. You will never begin a conversation. You will only reply when someone else speaks. Since you love to have the last word, I will give it to you. Never again will you speak words of your own. You may only repeat words that someone else has spoken."

"Spoken," said Echo. " . . . someone else has spoken."

Now the words of others were all that she could say.

Echo left the nymphs and went to live by herself in a corner of the forest where people seldom came. For a long time she did not speak at all.

One day a young hunter wandered by. Narcissus was his name, and he was extremely handsome. Echo watched him from behind the trees. She desperately wanted to speak to him, but she could not say one word until he spoke to her first.

Echo followed the handsome young man through the forest. After a time Narcissus noticed her. He smiled and called, "Hello! Who are you? What is your name?"

"What is your name . . . your name . . . your name . . . ," said Echo.

"My name is Narcissus," he answered. "I came to the forest to hunt deer. Now it's your turn to tell me your name."

"Tell me your name . . . name . . . name . . . ," Echo said.

"I've already told you. It's Narcissus. Didn't you hear me?"

"Hear me . . . me . . .
me . . . ," Echo answered.

Narcissus grew angry.
"Are you playing a joke? I don't
like it when people make fun of
me. If you want to talk, answer properly
when I speak to you. If not, go away."

"Go away . . . away . . . away . . . ," Echo said.
The poor nymph did not know what to do. How
could she explain to Narcissus that she could only
repeat the words he said?

Echo came from behind the trees.
She walked toward Narcissus, holding out

her arms. She hoped he would understand that she wanted to be his friend.

Narcissus did not understand at all. He thought Echo was laughing at him. "Don't tell me to go away. Go away yourself!" He pushed Echo hard. She fell down. Echo began to cry. Tears ran down her cheeks, but not a single sound came from her lips.

Narcissus cared not one bit about her tears. "Cry all you want. I don't care. You made fun of me. You got what you deserved." He slung his bow and arrows over his shoulder and walked away.

Echo tried to make him come back. She called to Narcissus. But the only words she could say were, "Got what you deserved . . . you deserved . . . you deserved. . . ."

Echo, heartbroken, began to fade. Slowly she disappeared

until she was no more than a shadow among the forest leaves. Then the shadow disappeared too. Nothing remained of Echo except her voice.

Echo's voice still lingers in the hills and mountains. If you hear a voice repeating your words, you'll know that she is there. We call that voice an *echo.*

And what of Narcissus? Artemis was angry with him for his cruelty to Echo. She made a spring appear in the forest where Narcissus would go to hunt. The spring's waters flowed like liquid silver. Its sparkling surface shone like a mirror.

Artemis dipped one of her arrows into the spring. She placed her magic in its waters. Whatever the spring reflected would appear to be ten times more beautiful than it really was.

Narcissus came upon the spring one afternoon. Hunting all day had left him tired and thirsty. He kneeled beside the spring to drink. What was this? He saw a face in the water. It was his own face, but Narcissus did not realize that. It seemed so lovely, so full of life. Narcissus fell in love with his own reflection. "Beautiful person, speak to me. Tell me your name."

The image on the water moved its lips, but it did not speak. Narcissus tried to kiss it. The image disappeared the moment his lips touched the spring.

Narcissus sighed.

"Although you will not

allow me to touch you, you cannot stop me from looking at you."

Narcissus sat by the spring, day after day, staring at his own beautiful reflection. He did not eat. He did not sleep. He grew weak and pale. His body wasted away. He felt himself dying, but he could not tear himself away from the spring.

"Alas!" he cried to his reflection. "If only you could see how much I love you."

Saying that, he died. Echo repeated his last words over and over again.

". . . how much I love you . . . how much I love you . . ."

The nymphs gathered to bury Narcissus. They could not find him. On the spot where he lay they saw a flower growing—a beautiful flower, like a golden trumpet surrounded by yellow petals.

The Greeks called this flower the *Narcissus,* after the poor young man who fell in love with himself. We see it in gardens every spring. We call it the *daffodil.*

ARACHNE

THERE WAS ONCE A YOUNG WOMAN named Arachne who loved to weave and spin. She could take the roughest fleece and card it into a pile of wool as light and fluffy as a cloud. Her spindle seemed to whirl by itself, spinning the fibers slipping through her fingers into a fine, even thread. When she wove, her shuttle danced across the loom.

Arachne's work was highly prized. One king paid its weight in gold for a cloak she wove for him. He wrapped it around his shoulders, saying, "I could not have a finer mantle if Athena herself were to weave it for me."

Arachne looked up from her loom. "Are you saying that Athena's work is better than mine? How do you know? When has anyone seen fabric woven by Athena?"

"Athena is the goddess of wisdom," the king replied. "She taught humans how to weave, sew, and spin. She invented these arts. How can anyone surpass her?"

"First does not mean best," Arachne answered. "I can weave and spin better than my mother, although I learned the art from her. If Athena's work is as good as everyone says, why do we never see it? Is she worried that it might not meet the test? Let Athena match

her work against mine. That will prove who is the better weaver."

The king hurried away, shocked by Arachne's words. An old woman sitting nearby shook her head.

"Dear child, take back this foolish talk. It is wrong to speak disrespectfully of Athena. Your skill at the loom is unsurpassed among human beings. However, the power of the gods is beyond anything we can imagine. No one can challenge the gods and win."

"That's what they want us to believe," Arachne said. "I am willing to match my skill against Athena's. Let the world see who is best. Let her take up my challenge—if she is not afraid."

"She is not afraid!" The old woman rose to her feet. She threw off her ragged cloak. Athena stood before Arachne in all her glory. She waved her spear. Two looms magically appeared.

"I accept your challenge," Athena said. "We will each weave a tapestry. A jury of gods and humans will judge who is the winner."

Arachne and Athena sat down before their looms and set to work.

Their fingers flew across the threads, filling their looms with brightly colored patterns.

Athena chose "The Heavens" as her theme. She wove the moon and the stars out of gold thread, set against a background of deep blue. The stars shimmered. The constellations seemed so lifelike that they appeared to move. Orion the Hunter strode across the sky with his club over his shoulders. The stars in his belt gleamed brightly. Scorpio the Scorpion raised his tail. Leo the Lion opened his jaws and roared. Taurus the Bull lowered his head to charge.

Athena rested from her work. She glanced over her shoulder to see what Arachne had woven.

Arachne chose "The Gods" as her theme. She filled her tapestry with pictures of all the foolish and cruel deeds the gods had done. Here was Prometheus chained to his rock with the vulture over his head. To his right was Ares, the god of war, rejoicing in slaughter. To his left was Aphrodite being married to Hephaestus, the scorched and ugly god of the forge.

Athena quivered with rage. Arachne's skill was almost equal to hers, but the girl's rudeness was inexcusable. Athena put down her shuttle. Turning to Arachne, she said, "You've proved your skill. I cannot allow this contest to continue, for it must never be said that a human defeated a god. If you agree, I will honor you with a gift."

"What is it?" Arachne asked.

"I will make you the greatest weaver who ever lived," Athena told her. "No one will surpass you. The threads you spin will be finer than silk and amazingly strong. In the early morning, when the dew is wet on the ground, your threads will sparkle with diamonds. You will never go hungry. Weaving will provide your food. You will pass your skill on to your daughters. They will all be great weavers, down through the genera-tions. All of this I promise. Do you accept?"

"I do!" Arachne said. Her eyes gleamed at the thought of receiving such a gift.

"It is yours," said Athena. She touched

Arachne's forehead with her shuttle. The young woman screamed as all the hair on her head came off, along with her nose and ears. Six more eyes popped out on her forehead. Two sets of arms and legs sprouted from her sides. She began to shrink until she became a tiny creature creeping along the ground. She climbed a tree and hung from a branch on a long, sticky thread that she spun from her own body.

Arachne had become a spider.

So Athena kept her promise, although not in the way that Arachne had imagined. Spiders are remarkable creatures. The threads that they spin are thinner than silk and incredibly strong. Spiders find their food in the juices that they suck from insects caught in their webs.

Morning dew on a spiderweb sparkles like diamonds in the sunlight.

And Arachne's daughters, the world's spiders, are all great weavers. Just like her.

PYGMALION AND GALATEA

PYGMALION WAS A SCULPTOR, the greatest in all of Greece. He created statues of marble, so skillfully formed that it seemed as if they might step down from their pedestals. Some swore they could see the statues breathe.

The priests of the temple at Paphos came to speak with Pygmalion. They asked him to carve a statue of Aphrodite. Pygmalion promised to create a statue worthy of Aphrodite and her temple.

Pygmalion selected a block of pure white marble. Tiny blue veins running through the stone made it look like human flesh. Pygmalion set to work. He hammered at the stone, day and night. He took no time to rest. It was as if the goddess were calling to him from inside the stone, crying to be let out.

"I will free you!" Pygmalion said, hammering away.

At last the statue was finished. Pygmalion put down his tools. He should have been happy. Instead he wept. Now he would have to summon the priests of Paphos. They would come to carry the statue away.

Pygmalion could not bear to part with it. It was the most beautiful statue he had ever created. Pygmalion placed a stool in front of the statue. He sat looking at it for hours.

The more he looked, the deeper in love he fell. He adored his own creation, even though she was made of stone. He called her Galatea, as if she were a living woman.

Pygmalion took his paint box. He painted Galatea's lips red and her eyes blue. The white marble of her hair became shining gold beneath his brush.

Now she seemed more lifelike than ever. Pygmalion dressed her in a robe of fine wool. He put rings on her fingers, bracelets around her wrists. He placed a gold necklace around her neck.

"Look at me! Speak to me!" Pygmalion pleaded. "Can't you see that I love you?"

Galatea's eyes never blinked. Her lips never moved. Pygmalion rose to embrace her. His arms closed around hard, cold stone.

The priests of Paphos came to Pygmalion again. Where was their statue? What was taking so long? Pygmalion promised that it would be finished soon.

Pygmalion found another block of marble. He set to work and created a second statue of Aphrodite. It was beautiful, to be sure—but not as beautiful as Galatea.

The priests of Paphos were pleased. They carried the statue off to their temple. Pygmalion kept his Galatea.

What was Pygmalion to do? Galatea was destroying him. He could not eat. He could not sleep. He spent days and nights staring at the woman he had created. Slowly he felt himself growing weaker. Pygmalion knew he was dying.

He threw himself down on his knees before Galatea. With the last of his strength he prayed to Aphrodite.

"Gracious Aphrodite, goddess of love and beauty, hear my voice. If Galatea can never be mine, take away my life. Let me find peace in death."

Pygmalion stretched out on the floor, waiting to die. Lying there, he felt a gentle hand touch his cheek. He looked up and found himself staring into the face of Galatea. She had come down from her pedestal. Her face shone with love.

Galatea was no longer a statue. She had become a living, breathing human being.

"Arise, Pygmalion," she said. "The goddess has answered our prayers. Your love was so great that it touched my heart, even though I was made of stone. Aphrodite has given me life, so that I may bring life and love to you."

Pygmalion and Galatea were soon married. Their love grew even stronger over the many years that they lived together. When Pygmalion and Galatea died, Aphrodite granted them a final blessing. Their souls left their bodies at the same time, so that they did not have to live even one moment apart.

KING MIDAS AND THE GOLDEN TOUCH

KING MIDAS OF PHRYGIA WAS the richest man on earth. Chests of gold, silver, and jewels filled his treasure house. Midas had more money than anyone could imagine, but it was not enough.

"More gold!" he muttered, sinking his arms elbow-deep into his coin chests.

"More jewels!" he exclaimed as rubies and diamonds ran through his fingers.

"More! More! More!" he shouted to the walls of his treasure house. The echo answered, "More!"

The god Dionysius happened to be walking by. He heard strange cries coming from the treasure house. He looked through the barred window and saw King Midas rolling in a great pile of gold coins. He looked like a pig wallowing in mud.

The ridiculous sight made Dionysius laugh. King Midas stopped rolling and looked up. "Are you laughing at me?" he asked.

"Of course I am," said Dionysius. "Don't you realize how silly you look?"

"I don't care what you think," Midas said. "I love money. I want as much as I can get."

"You should think less about getting and more about giving,"

Dionysius suggested. "Why not use your wealth to help poor, hungry people? Your money does no good lying in your treasure house. You may as well bury it in the ground."

"Give my money away? You must be mad!" Midas exclaimed. "I wish that everything I touch would turn to gold."

Dionysius shook his head. "Do you really think the Golden Touch would bring you happiness?"

"I know it would!" Midas answered.

"Let's find out." Dionysius whispered a secret word known only to the gods. Then he disappeared.

"What a strange fellow," Midas said. "Anyone who thinks that giving money away makes people happy must be crazy. I can't have crazy people wandering around my kingdom. I'll send some soldiers to lock him up."

Midas stepped outside his treasure house. He pulled the heavy door shut and locked it with an iron key. Suddenly the door began to shimmer. It grew so bright that Midas had to cover his eyes. When he opened them, he discovered something amazing.

The great oak and iron door had turned to gold. So had the key in his hand.

Midas danced along the path to his garden. "I have the Golden Touch!" he shouted. "The gods have granted my wish! I am the happiest man alive!"

Midas ran through his garden, touching the trees and flowers. They all turned to gold. So did the water in the pond, the frogs on the lily pads, and the fish swimming below in the cool depths.

Midas walked across the grass. He left golden footprints wherever he stepped as the green grass beneath his sandals turned to gold too.

Midas was so happy that he did not notice how his garden had changed. Gold flowers gave off no fragrance. The golden leaves of the trees rattled in the wind like a noisy tambourine. No fish splashed. No frogs croaked. Golden grass scratched Midas's ankles like sharp wire. All the colors of the garden had disappeared. There was only one color now: gold!

Midas ran off to his palace. He told his servants to prepare a feast to celebrate his good fortune. He summoned his family and friends to share the feast with him.

The servants brought tasty dishes from the kitchen. They brought jugs of rare wine up from the cellar. Midas lifted his wine cup. It turned to gold in his hand. Everyone at the table gasped.

"A toast to the richest king on earth, who is about to become richer!" said Midas.

"To the king," everyone at the table replied. They all drank. Except for Midas. As soon as the wine touched his lips, it turned to gold.

He set his cup aside. "Let the feast begin," he ordered. The guests began eating. Midas tried to eat too. But every morsel that entered his mouth turned to gold.

Midas's cat, Niobe, jumped onto his lap. At once she turned to gold. His dog, Ajax, nuzzled his hand. As soon as the dog touched his master's fingers, he also turned to gold.

A look of horror crossed Midas's face. The guests stared at the king. No one knew what to do. Phoebe, Midas's daughter, rose from her seat. "Father, what is wrong? Are you ill?" she asked. Before Midas could stop her, she placed her hand on his forehead. Instantly, like the cat and the dog, she turned into a golden statue.

Midas threw himself from his chair. He rolled on the floor, moaning. "I am the richest of kings, and the poorest of humankind. Now I understand what the gods meant to teach me. The Golden Touch is a curse, not a blessing. It has destroyed my daughter and the creatures that were dear to me. What use is my wealth? It cannot buy me a cup of cold water or a crust of dry bread. Now I know what it means to be hungry, thirsty, frightened, and alone. Too late, I have learned what is really important. Better that I had been a good man instead of a rich one!"

"You were always a good man. Your eyes were blinded by the glitter of gold," a voice said. Midas looked up. Dionysius stood before him in all his glory.

Midas bowed to the god. "Forgive me for my greed. Forgive me for caring only about myself."

"You have learned your lesson. There is no reason to torture you." Dionysius whispered the secret word, and the air shimmered with the colors of the rainbow.

Midas shut his eyes. When he opened them, he found himself sitting at his feast. Phoebe stood at his side, telling him about an adventure she'd had with her friends. Ajax nuzzled his hand. Niobe sat purring in his lap.

"Bring me a cup of water. And some bread," Midas said. Never had food or drink tasted so good. He touched the trays, the napkins, the tablecloth. He sighed with relief. Nothing turned to gold. A breeze from the garden carried the fragrance of roses through the window.

The Golden Touch was gone forever.

"Throw open the doors of my palace," Midas said. "Invite everyone in the kingdom to share my feast. Unlock my treasure house. Give the poor people whatever they need."

From that day on, no one in Midas's kingdom went without food, clothing, or a place to live. The king gave away money to all who needed it.

Midas was no longer the richest king on earth, but he was surely the most beloved. That made him richer still.

ORPHEUS AND EURYDICE

WHEN ORPHEUS WAS A LITTLE BOY, he received a lyre from Apollo, the sun god. The nine Muses, the spirits of art and poetry, taught Orpheus how to play. Orpheus fell in love with music. He sat in the forest, hour after hour, practicing on his lyre.

Soon Orpheus played well enough to create his own songs. They were so beautiful that farmers stopped plowing their fields to listen. Shepherds stopped herding their flocks. Even fishermen far out on the ocean stopped pulling in their nets to listen as the wind carried Orpheus's sweet songs across the waves.

Animals, too, came to listen. Wolves, bears, and lions emerged from the forest when Orpheus sang. They sat beside him with their heads in his lap. Snakes twined around his feet. Even trees and rocks began to dance as Orpheus played.

When Orpheus grew up, he took part in a great adventure called the Quest for the Golden Fleece. Soon after his return he fell in love.

Eurydice was the young woman's name. She was a kind, gentle person who lived in the forest. Eurydice knew all of Orpheus's songs by heart. She and Orpheus would sing them together. Their love for each other made the songs even more beautiful.

They held their wedding in an ancient temple. Apollo and the Muses came. As the ceremony began, all the torches began to sputter. Smoke filled the temple, stinging the eyes of the guests. They began to weep.

Tears at a wedding were a terrible omen. They meant that a dreadful fate awaited the happy couple.

The omen proved true. Eurydice was walking through the forest when a snake bit her ankle. Poison rushed through her veins, and she fell down on a pile of leaves. By the time Orpheus found her, she had died. Her spirit flew down to the Underworld to join the souls of the dead.

Heartbroken, Orpheus vowed to follow her. "I will go down to the realm of the dead. I will find my bride and bring her back."

Orpheus journeyed to the cave that led to the Underworld. He forced his way through crowds of spirits waiting to cross the River Styx.

"Go back! No living being can come here!" shouted Charon, the ferryman of the dead. Cerberus, the three-headed watchdog, bared his teeth and growled.

Orpheus, unafraid, took up his lyre and began to play. He sang of his love for Eurydice and how much he missed her. Orpheus's song brought tears to Charon's eyes. Cerberus threw back his three heads and howled. The spirits of the dead, who had left behind all feelings of love, joy, and sorrow, began to weep.

"I will take you across," said Charon. "You may speak to Hades, our king, and his wife, Persephone. Let them decide what is to be."

Orpheus sang and played his lyre as he walked through the dark passages. Cries and groans ceased as the whole Underworld paused to listen.

Orpheus came before Hades, the lord of the dead. "I have come to plead for my bride, Eurydice," he said. "Her life was cut short. I cannot bear to be apart from her. Have pity on us. Let me take her back to the land of the living. If not, allow me to remain here in your kingdom, so that we may be together."

"I cannot help you," said Hades. "You are still alive. Living souls cannot remain here. Your bride, Eurydice, is dead. The dead can never return to those they left behind."

Orpheus began to weep. He took up his lyre and began to play, turning his sorrow into song.

Am I alive, dreaming of death?
Or am I dead, dreaming of life?
No place is there for me in the land of the departed.
No place do I have in the land of the living.
Eurydice is gone, and I am lost without her.

Tears ran down the face of grim Hades. The stone walls of the caverns trembled as the lord of the Underworld wept. Tears flowed from the eyes of Persephone, his queen. As Orpheus's song ended, Persephone spoke.

"You are wrong, my husband," she said to Hades. "Do I not return to the world of the living every year? Take pity on Orpheus and his bride. What have we to lose? They will live out their lives and return to us eventually. Let them taste of joy and love while they can."

Her words melted the heart of Hades. "Summon the spirit of Eurydice," he commanded. Eurydice's spirit came forward from among the crowd

of dead souls. She limped on the wounded foot that the snake had bitten. Her pale face brightened when she saw Orpheus.

"Is that you, my beloved Orpheus?" she cried.

"Yes," Orpheus said. "I have come to bring you back from the dead."

"Take Eurydice with you to the world above," Hades told Orpheus. "Walk before her. She will follow. Remember: You must not turn around to look at her until you both reach the upper world. If you so much as glance at Eurydice while you are still within my kingdom, her spirit will return to the realm of the dead, never to depart."

With Persephone's blessing, Orpheus and Eurydice set out on the path that would lead them to the land of the living. Orpheus walked ahead. Eurydice followed behind.

Crowds of dead souls parted to let them pass. Charon, the ferryman, was waiting. He carried them to the river's opposite shore. Cerberus wagged his tail. He licked Orpheus's hand as he passed.

Orpheus never spoke a word to Eurydice throughout their long journey. He walked silently through the shadows, never stopping to look back. One by one he climbed the steep steps that led to the mouth of the cave. He rushed into the sunlight.

"We are here, Eurydice! You have come back to life again!" Orpheus shouted. He turned around to see his bride.

Alas! He had spoken too soon. Eurydice was still standing inside the cave. One step more and she would have been in the sunlight.

Too late! Orpheus caught a final glimpse of Eurydice's loving face. She called to him, but he could not hear her words. Then she disappeared.

Broken with sorrow, Orpheus hid himself in the deepest part of the forest. Day and night he wept as he played his lyre, singing for his lost Eurydice. A tribe of wild maidens heard his voice.

"He's beautiful!" one savage maiden murmured. "And he sings so sweetly. I want him for my husband."

"No, I saw him first! He is mine!"

"I can be no one's husband," Orpheus told them. "My heart belongs to Eurydice, and she is gone forever. I cannot love another. I have no love to give."

His words enraged the maidens. "We don't ask for your love! We take what we want. And we want you!"

Orpheus ignored them. He picked up his lyre and began to play.

"Do you turn your back on us? How dare you!" One maiden picked up a javelin and hurled it at Orpheus. The power of his music protected him. The javelin fell at his feet.

The maidens shot arrows and hurled spears. None of their weapons could hurt Orpheus. He continued playing his lyre and singing for his lost Eurydice.

The maidens tore at their hair. They scratched their faces until blood ran down their cheeks. They screamed and howled like wild animals. Their cries drowned out the sound of Orpheus's music. It no longer had the power to protect him.

Again the maidens hurled their weapons at Orpheus. This time the spears and arrows found their mark. Orpheus fell dead, pierced with a hundred wounds. The maidens tore his body to pieces and threw the fragments in the river, along with the broken lyre.

Apollo found the lyre floating in the water. He placed it in the heavens with the other constellations, in memory of Orpheus. It still shines in the night sky today.

Orpheus is gone. But do not weep for him. His spirit returned to the Underworld, to his beloved Eurydice. Their two souls are together at last, never to be parted.

JASON AND THE GOLDEN FLEECE

KING AESON OF THESSALY GREW tired of being a king. He gave his crown to his brother, Pelias, on one condition: When Aeson's son, Jason, became old enough to rule, Pelias would return the crown to him.

However, when Jason grew up, his uncle was unwilling to step aside. "You are still not ready," Pelias told Jason. "You need to perform a great deed. Do something to prove you are worthy."

"I know what I can do," said Jason. "I will bring back the Golden Fleece from the land of Colchis. No one would challenge my right to rule if I were to do that."

Jason summoned the bravest young men in Greece to join him. Some became heroes of legend. Theseus arrived, as did Orpheus and Heracles. So many answered the call that Jason had to build a special ship to carry them. He named the ship *Argo*. He and his companions called themselves the "Argonauts."

After many adventures the Argonauts arrived in Colchis. They anchored in the harbor and went ashore to pay their respects to Aeëtes, the king.

"I have come to bring the Golden Fleece back to my country, to prove that I am worthy of being king," Jason told Aeëtes.

"You are welcome to try," Aeëtes said. "Many have come before you. They all paid with their lives. You must face the same challenges that they did. I have two fire-breathing bulls with brass hooves in my stable. Your first task is to harness both to a plow and sow the dragon's teeth."

"I am not afraid," said Jason. "I will meet every challenge and overcome them all."

The people of Colchis gathered on the hillsides to watch. The Argonauts feared for Jason. They wanted to help, but they knew he had to face the challenges alone.

The bulls came rushing out. They tore up the ground with their horns and burned the grass with their fiery breath. Their

brass hooves clattered over the stones. Jason took a handful of grain as he walked toward them. He spoke gently, without fear. As the bulls came closer to smell the grain, he stroked their heads and scratched them between their ears.

The bulls stopped stamping and snorting. They allowed Jason to place the yoke on their shoulders. He hitched them to the plow. The bulls pulled the plow back and forth across the field, following Jason's commands as if they were tame oxen.

The Argonauts and the people of Colchis cheered for Jason. Aeëtes came forward and handed him a leather sack. "You have passed the first test," he said. "Now for the second. Are you ready to sow the dragon's teeth?"

"I am," said Jason. He took the sack and prepared to begin. Suddenly a voice cried, "Stop!"

It was Medea, Aeëtes' daughter. Jason's good looks had caught her eye when he arrived in Colchis. Now his courage had won her heart.

"He is so brave! I want to wish him good luck," Medea told her father.

"Do as you please, but don't be long about it," said Aeëtes.

Medea threw her arms around Jason's neck and pretended to kiss him. At the same time she whispered in his ear, "You can never succeed—unless you have this!" She pressed a small stone into his hand. "It is a magic charm. Dragon warriors will come out of the ground. Fight them as long as you can. When you feel yourself weakening, throw this charm into their midst." Medea was a sorcerer who could call on powerful forces. "I can help you win the Golden Fleece," she said, "if you promise to take me with you when you sail for home."

"I promise," Jason whispered.

He walked across the plowed fields, casting handfuls of the dragon's teeth between the furrows. The ground began to tremble as armored men sprouted from the earth. These dragon warriors drew their swords and rushed to attack Jason.

Jason fought back. For every warrior he killed, two more arose to take his place. Jason felt himself tiring. He could not fight much longer.

"Now is the time, Jason!" Medea cried.

Jason heard her voice over the screams of battle. He threw her charm into the middle of the dragon warriors. At once they turned away from Jason and began to fight one another. They hacked away until all lay dead on the field.

"Only one test remains," said Aeëtes. "In
the morning you will meet the dragon and see if
you can take the Golden Fleece from him."

However, Medea had other plans. She went to meet
Jason in the dead of night. "You cannot wait until morning,"
she warned him. "My father will never allow you to leave his
kingdom. And you have little hope of overcoming the dragon
unless I help you."

"What must I do?" Jason asked.

"Tell your companions to prepare the *Argo* to sail. Make
sure they are all aboard. All I ask is that you remember your
promise. When you leave, take me with you."

"I surely will," said Jason.

Medea handed him a small glass bottle. "Now is
the time to face the dragon. Hurl this bottle at his head.
There is a potion inside that will make him sleepy. You can
take the Golden Fleece as soon as he closes his eyes."

Jason awakened his companions and told them to
get ready. Medea would stay with them aboard
the *Argo*. Meanwhile, Jason took
the bottle and found his way in the

dark to the sacred forest. The full moon, sacred to Hecate, ruler of the forces of magic and witchcraft, lit his way.

Jason saw the dragon stalking among the trees. He saw the Golden Fleece hanging in the branches of an enormous oak. It sparkled in the moonlight.

Jason stepped from the shadows. As the dragon rushed at him, Jason hurled the bottle at its head. The delicate glass shattered, and the dragon stopped in its tracks. Its eyes began to close. The dragon lowered its head to the ground and fell fast asleep.

Jason pulled the Golden Fleece down from the oak. Wrapping it around his shoulders, he ran to join his companions.

Jason leaped aboard as the Argonauts pulled up the anchor. Medea summoned a wind that filled the sail. But they did not leave the harbor unnoticed. One of the watchmen sent word to Aeëtes. The king set out after Jason in a swift war galley.

Medea stood in the stern, watching in the moonlight as her father's ship came closer. She turned her face to the full moon and spoke these words.

"Great Hecate, ruler of the darkness, I summon you." The stars

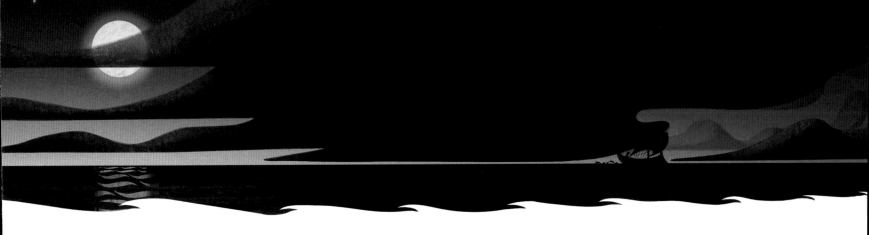

went out. The shining moon turned black. A dense cloud enveloped the *Argo*. When the cloud lifted, Aeëtes' ship was gone. The *Argo* was hundreds of miles away.

The Argonauts returned to Thessaly. The people celebrated their return with a great festival. Yet Jason could not rejoice. Aeson, his father, lay dying.

"Is there nothing you can do?" Jason asked Medea.

"I can make him young again," Medea answered. "But only if you have the courage to do what must be done."

"I will do whatever you ask," Jason promised.

Medea built an altar of stones. That night, while Jason and his father looked on, Medea sacrificed a black ram to Hecate. She set a cauldron on the fire. As it began to boil, she danced around it, tossing in herbs, stones, and magic charms.

"Great Hecate," she cried. "I, your servant Medea, call to you. Fill my potion with your power. Turn weakness into strength, old age into youth, death into life!" She took a dry olive branch and dipped it into the bubbling cauldron. When she drew it out, the branch was green, covered with leaves and ripe olives.

Medea handed Jason a knife. "Now is the time. Kill your father!" she commanded.

Jason refused. "How can I do such a terrible thing?"

Medea's eyes flashed with anger. "You are weak. You said you had the courage to do what must be done. If you cannot do it, I can!"

She snatched the knife away and killed Aeson. After draining the old man's blood, she picked him up and placed him into the cauldron. She stirred the magic brew three times with the olive branch. After the third time she pulled Aeson out of the cauldron and laid him on the earth.

Jason saw his father transformed before his eyes. Aeson's snow-white hair turned black. His missing teeth grew back. The muscles of his arms and legs swelled with strength. Aeson rose from the ground. The old man had become young again.

Jason kneeled before his father. "Take back your throne. You should be king."

"No, my son. I am done with being king," Aeson said. "It is your turn now. I will demand that Pelias give you the crown."

Jason took Medea's hand. "When I am king, you will be my queen."

Medea pushed him away. "You did not have the courage to do as I asked. You are a coward, like all men. I do not need a husband.

I do not need any man. I am wiser and more powerful than all the men who ever lived."

The next night Pelias's daughters came to Medea. "Our father is old and weak, but he is still king. We do not want to give up the throne to Jason. Help us, Medea. Make Pelias young again, so we can keep the crown."

Medea promised to help Pelias's daughters. She led them to the place where she had built the altar. Pelias was too weak to walk by himself. His daughters carried him. Medea kindled a fire. She sacrificed another ram and set the cauldron boiling.

As the potion bubbled, Medea handed Pelias's oldest daughter a knife. "You know what to do," she said. The young woman plunged the knife into her father's body.

"Give me the knife! I am just as strong as my sister." Pelias's second daughter took the knife and stabbed him again. The two daughters lifted Pelias up and dropped him into the cauldron.

Medea gave Pelias's daughters an olive branch. "Stir the cauldron with this. Don't stop until I tell you."

As they stirred, Medea prayed silently to Hecate. "Mother of Darkness, take me away from this place. I want no more to do with treacherous, cowardly people."

A chariot drawn by snakes appeared. Medea stepped inside. The chariot flew up into the night sky and disappeared.

What of Pelias's daughters? They stirred and stirred the cauldron as Medea ordered, hoping to bring their father back to life. If they haven't stopped stirring by now, they're stirring still.

DAEDALUS AND ICARUS

DAEDALUS OF ATHENS WAS the first great inventor. He invented the saw, the potter's wheel, and the compass for drawing circles. Many of his inventions are still used today.

Daedalus became known throughout the world. Minos, the king of Crete, invited him to Knossos, the capital of his kingdom. There Daedalus built a royal palace whose ruins can still be seen. It was one of the largest, most beautiful buildings in the ancient world.

Daedalus also built a labyrinth beneath Minos's palace. The labyrinth was a network of tunnels and passages that twisted and turned in every direction. It was a perfect place to keep treasures. It was also a perfect place to keep people and creatures that Minos did not want to be seen.

People who entered the labyrinth would never find their way out again unless they possessed the magic key. The key was a ball of thread. They tied it to the entrance and rolled it into the labyrinth. The thread led them through the tunnels to wherever they wanted to go. To go out, they followed the thread back to the entrance.

Daedalus had invented this magic ball of thread. He had only made one, which he gave to Minos. How pleased Minos was with Daedalus's gift!

"You must stay with me in Knossos as my honored guest," he said.

Minos gave money to Daedalus to build his own palace. He gave him one of his daughters to be his wife. Her name was Naucrate. Daedalus loved her very much. Together they had a son, whom they named Icarus.

Icarus grew up to become a handsome young man. Minos made sure that Daedalus and his family had everything they wanted.

Then Naucrate died. Daedalus began longing to return to Greece. He hadn't seen his native city of Athens for twenty years. Icarus was eager to go too. His father had told him stories about the world beyond Crete's little island. Icarus wanted to see these places for himself.

Daedalus asked Minos for permission to leave. The king refused. He did not want the greatest inventor in the world to work for anyone else. He locked Daedalus and Icarus inside the labyrinth to teach them a lesson.

"Don't ever try to leave Crete," he warned when he released them. "If I discover you're planning to escape, I'll put you both in the labyrinth for good."

Daedalus was frightened, but he was not ready to submit. He climbed to the roof of his palace to think. He looked down at the ships anchored in the bay. There could be no escape by sea. Minos's soldiers controlled the harbor. They patrolled every inch of the seashore. If Daedalus and Icarus could not leave by water, how else could they get away?

While Daedalus thought about the problem, he noticed a flock of seagulls flying overhead. The squawking gulls seemed to be laughing at him.

"Laugh if you like, you silly birds," Daedalus said. "You think getting off this island is easy. It is for you. You can fly." Suddenly Daedalus had an idea.

For the next several months he studied the birds. He watched as they flew around the island. He discovered how warm air rising from the sea carried them higher. He examined dead birds to learn how feathers, bones, and muscles came together to form a wing. Daedalus began scratching designs on a wax tablet. He and Icarus walked along the seashore, collecting feathers from dead birds.

Minos soon learned what they were doing. He ordered that Daedalus and Icarus be brought to him.

"What are you up to?" he asked. "Tell me the truth or I'll put you both back in the labyrinth."

"I'm going to build a pair of wings for Icarus and myself," Daedalus answered. "We're going to learn how to fly."

How Minos laughed! "What a foolish idea! People can't fly! Flying is for birds!"

"People can do anything if they think long and hard about it," Daedalus replied.

Minos dismissed them. "Go ahead! Make all the wings you like. You'll never escape from Crete that way."

Daedalus only smiled. He bowed and went back to his work room.

Daedalus made two pairs of wings. The frames were wood and wire, covered with wax. Daedalus stuck the feathers into the wax when it was soft. The wax would hold them in place when it hardened.

Daedalus and Icarus chose a day when a strong breeze blew from the mountains to the ocean. They carried their wings up to the roof and strapped them on.

"Hold out your arms," Daedalus told his son. "Pretend you are a bird. Let the air carry you. Don't tire yourself out by flapping too much."

Icarus felt so excited that he barely heard Daedalus's last warning: "Remember to not fly near the sun. The wax on your wings will melt. The feathers will come loose. You will fall into the sea."

"I'm ready, Father," said Icarus. "May I go first?"

"Go ahead," said Daedalus. "Lead the way. I will follow."

Icarus stepped onto the balcony. He climbed on top of the wall and leaped into space. Daedalus gasped as he saw his son falling. But then his wings caught the air. Up, up, flew Icarus. Daedalus watched him soar higher and higher, until he was a dot in the sky.

Now came Daedalus's turn. He leaped from the balcony. The air lifted him up. He tried his wings. They carried him perfectly.

The gulls flew by to have a look. "What is this strange new bird?" they seemed to call to each other. Daedalus looked up. He saw Icarus flying toward the roof of the sky. "Where is that boy going?" he muttered. "He is much too high. He must not go near the sun." Daedalus raised his voice. "Icarus! Come back!"

But Icarus was too far away to hear. He flew even higher into the clear, blue sky, entranced at being so close to heaven. Looking down, he saw the mighty ocean. It seemed no more than a puddle. The great city of Cnossos looked like an anthill. Icarus turned his eyes upward. *I want to fly higher,* he told himself. *I want to see what the gods see!*

He did not notice how close he was coming to the sun. He did not see the wax of his wings beginning to melt.

"Come back, Icarus!" Daedalus shouted one last time. A feather floated down past his face. Then another. And another.

"Icarus!" Daedalus screamed as his son toppled out of the sky.

"Father! Help me!" Icarus cried as he tumbled down, down, down.

It was too late. Hovering in the air, Daedalus could only watch helplessly as his son plunged into the sea.

Daedalus flew down. He pulled Icarus's broken body from the waves. He carried him to a nearby island. There he buried his son on the highest peak, as close to heaven as he could bring him. The island is still called Icaria, in honor of Icarus, the boy who soared with the birds.

THESEUS AND THE MINOTAUR

MINOS WAS OUTRAGED TO LEARN that Daedalus and Icarus had escaped. Since Daedalus was an Athenian, Minos decided to punish the people of Athens.

Minos possessed a vast collection of birds and animals that his ships had brought to Crete from all over the world. One creature was too fierce to keep in an ordinary cage. This was the Minotaur, a monster with a man's body and a bull's head.

The Minotaur fed on human flesh. It killed anyone who came near. Minos kept the monster in the labyrinth that Daedalus had built beneath the royal palace. The creature guarded Minos's treasure. What thief would dare enter the labyrinth, knowing that the Minotaur lurked in its tunnels?

As punishment for the escape of Daedalus and Icarus, Minos decreed that every year the city of Athens was to send seven of its most beautiful young women and seven of its handsomest young men to Crete. When they arrived, they would be thrust into the labyrinth to be devoured by the Minotaur.

Year after year a ship with black sails carried the unfortunate victims to Crete. The Athenians wept to know that their sons and daughters were going to be eaten by a monster. They also wept for shame, knowing that they were too weak to save them. Minos possessed a powerful army. No city in the world could stand against the Cretans.

Aegeus was the king of Athens. His son, Theseus, watched the black-sailed ships leave the harbor year after year. He clenched his fists with rage, seeing the cowardliness of the Athenians.

"How much longer will we be slaves to the Cretans?" Theseus asked his father.

"If we defy Minos, he will burn our city to the ground," Aegeus answered. "It is better to sacrifice a few young people to the Minotaur so that the rest of us can live."

"Then sacrifice me," Theseus said. "Why should the king's son remain at home while other families are asked to give up their children?"

"You do not know what you are asking," Aegeus cried. "You are my only son. Who will be king after me if you meet your death in the labyrinth?"

"I do not intend to die," Theseus said. "I am going to kill the Minotaur."

On the day the ship set sail, Aegeus asked his son, "How will I know if you succeed?"

Theseus told his father, "Look at the ship's sails as it enters the harbor. If I am dead, the captain will hoist black sails. If I am alive, the sails will be white. White sails mean that I overcame the monster and am on my way home."

Aegeus kissed his son as he boarded the ship with the other unlucky young men and women bound for Crete. "May the gods protect Theseus and all the others," Aegeus murmured as he watched the black sails sinking below the horizon.

The ship arrived in Crete. Theseus and his companions were led before Minos. "Would any of you like to beg for mercy?" the king asked.

"You never granted mercy before," said Theseus. "Why would you grant it now? Better for us to die on our feet as heroes than live as cowards on our knees."

Theseus's companions cheered. His words gave them courage. They were ready to face death with him.

"You will have your wish," said Minos. "Tomorrow you will go into the labyrinth. We will see how brave you are when you meet the Minotaur."

Minos's daughter, Ariadne, had been watching from behind a tapestry. She hated her father's cruelty, but she did not know how to stand against it. Theseus's words gave her courage. She thought of a way to save his life.

That night, while everyone in the palace slept, Ariadne crept through the dark corridors to the dungeon that held Theseus and his companions.

"Theseus, son of Aegeus, are you there?" she whispered.

"Who speaks?" Theseus asked.

"A friend," Ariadne answered. She thrust a bundle through the bars in the door. "If you wish to save your life and the lives of your friends, listen carefully to my words. A spool of thread and a sword are inside this bundle. Carry them with you when you enter the labyrinth tomorrow. Tie the thread to the entrance of the tunnel. It will lead you into the labyrinth. Follow it back when you come out again. A magic force protects the Minotaur. Only this sword can kill it. Be brave, and may the gods protect you!"

"Who are you?" Theseus asked. "What is your name?"

"I am Minos's daughter," she told him. "My name is Ariadne."

Theseus and his companions entered the labyrinth before dawn. Minos's guards marched them to the entrance and drove them in with the points of their spears. Theseus carried the sword and spool concealed beneath his cloak. When the guards couldn't see him, he tied one end of the thread to a rusty spike hammered into the wall. He tossed the spool into the dark cavern.

Theseus and his companions followed the thread deep into the labyrinth. Their torches' dim light revealed heaps of bones. Theseus recognized the clothes of friends who had sailed to Crete the year before.

"The Minotaur must be near," he told his companions. He drew the sword from beneath his cloak.

A roar filled the cavern. An immense shape appeared, blocking the path ahead. The creature's eyes glowed in the dark. Two mighty horns rose above its head. Theseus felt its hot breath on his face.

"I'm not afraid of you!" Theseus shouted. "If you want a fight, you'll have one. Come on! I'm ready!"

Theseus stabbed at the monster. The Minotaur bellowed with rage. Theseus swung his sword at the Minotaur with all his strength. Again and again he thrust. Finally a scream shook the cavern walls. Theseus felt hot blood gush over his body. The creature choked, gasped, then fell down dead.

"I have killed the Minotaur!" said Theseus. He cut off the

monster's head with one stroke. "We will carry this back to Athens," he told his companions. "We will hang it in the Temple of Athena to thank her for protecting us and bringing us safely home."

Theseus and his companions followed the thread through the labyrinth. It led them back to the entrance, where Ariadne awaited them.

"Hurry!" she told the Athenians. "You must be aboard your ship before my father finds out you have killed the Minotaur."

"Farewell, Ariadne!" said Theseus. "We will never forget your kindness."

"My father will put me to death when he finds out that I helped you," Ariadne said. "My life is in your hands, Theseus. Take me with you."

Theseus took Ariadne's hand. Together they boarded the ship for Athens.

When Minos learned that the Minotaur was dead and his daughter was missing, he sent out his fleet to bring back the black-sailed ship. But it was too late. The Athenians were long gone, carrying Ariadne with them.

Athena sent fair winds for the journey home. Theseus's ship sped across the ocean. It stopped at the island of Naxos to take on food and water. As the sailors worked, Theseus and Ariadne went for a walk along the shore.

"I am so happy," Ariadne said to Theseus. "I can hardly wait for us to return to Athens, so we can start planning our wedding."

Wedding? Theseus stopped in his tracks. He didn't want to marry Ariadne. It didn't matter that she had risked her life to save him. What mattered was that she had no wealth to bring to the marriage. Theseus wanted a bride who could make him rich.

Ariadne lay down to take a nap. Once she was asleep, Theseus ran back to the ship. The Athenians immediately set sail, abandoning Ariadne on the beach.

Athena, looking down from Mount Olympus, saw the cowardly trick that Theseus had played on Ariadne. "She saved him from the Minotaur, and this is how he thanks her," Athena said. "Ariadne will weep when she awakes. Theseus will weep too when he returns to Athens. I will make sure of that."

Athena cast a forgetting spell over the ship, causing a cloud to cover one important detail in Theseus's mind.

After a voyage of many weeks the ship sailed into the harbor at Athens. Aegeus sat watching from the cliffs. "There it is!" he cried when he saw the ship that had sailed for Crete. He strained to see the color of its sails. They were black.

"My son is gone, with all his companions!" Aegeus wailed. He hurled himself from the cliff into the sea. Theseus saw him fall.

"My father!" he shrieked. Then he remembered what Athena had caused him to forget until it was too late. He had not changed the ship's sails. They were still black.

Athena's words came true. Theseus wept for his father as Ariadne had wept for him.

What became of Ariadne? She found someone who loved her for her kindness and courage. He was a much better husband than Theseus could ever have been.

She married the god Dionysius.

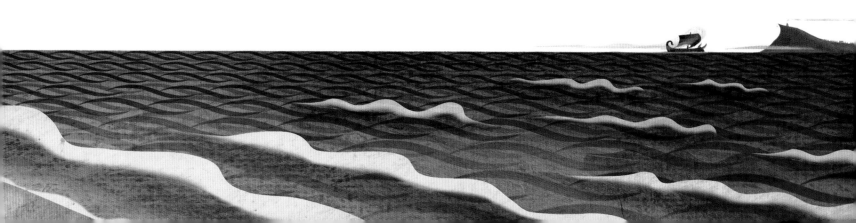

PERSEUS AND MEDUSA

PERSEUS WAS THE SON OF ZEUS, the ruler of the gods. When Perseus became a young man, he set out on a quest. He wanted to prove himself worthy of his father by winning fame and glory.

Perseus came to the land of Seriphus. He found the whole country blasted and barren. Nothing grew in the fields. The trees of the forests were blackened stumps. The people huddled in caves, afraid to come out. The only buildings that Perseus could see were burnt-out ruins.

"What has happened to your land?" he asked the king.

"My country is cursed by a monster," the king explained. "Her name is Medusa. Once she was a maiden who boasted of her beauty. The gods overheard her bragging and sent her a terrible punishment. They turned her tresses into a nest of writhing snakes. Beautiful Medusa became a frightening ogre. One glimpse of her is enough to turn a person to stone. Look around! You can see what she has done to my country. Have pity on us, Perseus! Rid us of this monster."

Perseus promised to do his best or die in the attempt. How was he to find Medusa? How was he to kill her when he could not even look at her?

Perseus offered a sacrifice to the gods. He prayed that they

86

would send him an answer. The gods heard his prayer. Athena and Hermes came down from Mount Olympus to help him.

"I will lend you my winged sandals," said Hermes. "They will carry you through the air to Medusa's cave."

"And I will lend you my shield," Athena added. "See how brightly it shines! Use it as a mirror when you fight Medusa. Do not look at her or you will turn to stone. Watch her reflection in the shield. It will show you where to strike with your sword."

Perseus thanked Athena and Hermes for their kindness. He tied Hermes' sandals around his ankles. He buckled Athena's shield over his left arm. Taking his sword in his right hand, he cried, "Carry me to Medusa!"

The wings on the sandals fluttered. They carried Perseus high into the sky and across the land of Seriphus. Perseus saw a range of mountains below. Smoke billowed from a cave. Perseus flew down to see what was inside. He passed over heaps of statues.

Suddenly he realized what they were. These were the bodies of people who had come to fight Medusa. She had turned them all to stone.

Perseus adjusted his shield so that he could see the mouth of the cave in the shield's mirrorlike surface. With his eyes fixed on the shield, he cried, "Medusa! It is I, Perseus, son of Zeus! I challenge you to fight!"

A rattling hiss filled the air as the monster emerged from her

cave. Her hair was a twisting, twining mass of snakes. Green scales covered her body from head to foot. Poison dripped from her fangs as she gnashed her teeth. She bared her claws.

"Perseus, son of Zeus!" she hissed. "Is that your name? I cannot remember the names of all who come to challenge me. But I remember their faces. I can see them now—as if they were carved in stone!" Medusa laughed long and hard. Smoke poured from her nostrils. She spit jets of flame at Perseus. His winged sandals carried him out of the way.

"Why don't you look at me, Perseus?" Medusa said. "Are you afraid of being overcome by my beauty?"

"Overcome, yes. By your beauty? No!" Perseus replied. "Take a look at yourself, but be careful. The sight of your own face might turn you to stone!"

Perseus turned his shield so that Medusa could see her own reflection. The monster shrieked. The writhing snakes spit poison. "How dare you laugh at me!" Medusa shouted. "I was beautiful once. I will be beautiful again!"

"You won't have the chance." Perseus fixed his eyes on Medusa's face, mirrored in the shining

shield. He gripped
his sword—and struck! Medusa's head flew
from her shoulders. Her curses died on
her lips. Her eyes, filled with hate, stayed
open, glaring at Perseus. One by one the
snakes of her hair lay still.

Even in death, Medusa's terrible face
still had the power to turn people to
stone. Perseus took care not to look
at it. He turned his eyes away as he
picked up the head and placed
it inside a leather sack.

Then he flew on, far out over the ocean, to the shores of the great sea. A large rock rose from the waves. Suddenly Perseus heard someone screaming for help. He flew down to see who it was.

He found a beautiful maiden chained to the rock. "Who are you?" Perseus asked. "What brought you here?"

"My name is Andromeda," the maiden told him. "My father's name is Cepheus. He is king of this country. My mother is Cassiopeia. She angered the gods by boasting of her beauty. They sent a dragon to destroy the cities of our coast. The monster has devoured whole towns. Hundreds of people have lost their lives. My parents asked the gods to forgive them. They begged them to save us from the dragon."

"What answer did the gods give?" Perseus asked.

"They told my father to sacrifice his daughter to the dragon," Andromeda said. "My parents did not want to do it, but they had no choice. Our people

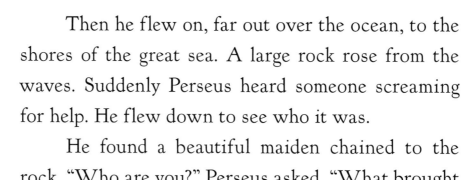

were suffering. They brought me to this rock. Now I wait for the dragon to come."

"Do not fear," said Perseus. "I will save you. When will the dragon arrive?"

"He is here now!" Andromeda screamed. Perseus turned in time to see a huge head rising from the sea. Barnacles grew on its scales. Seaweed dripped from its jaws.

The dragon lunged at Perseus, but Perseus's winged sandals carried him high in the air to safety. Perseus reached for Medusa's head in the leather bag. *I cannot let this creature hurt Andromeda,* he thought. *I can easily turn it to stone by showing it Medusa's head. But if I do, the victory will never really be mine. I must defeat this dragon myself, relying only on my courage.*

Perseus drew his sword. He flew down to attack the dragon. Again and again he stabbed at the creature.

He felt like a bee trying to fight an elephant. The dragon breathed fire at Perseus. Perseus covered himself with Athena's shield just in time.

The fight continued for hours. Andromeda begged Perseus to flee. She told him that the dragon was too strong. No one could help her. But Perseus refused to run away. "If I cannot save you, we will die together," he vowed.

Perseus felt himself growing tired. The dragon's scales were like bronze armor. There seemed no way for his sword to penetrate them. Suddenly he noticed a spot beneath the dragon's neck where his scales did not quite grow together. The opening was no wider than a fingertip. Would it be enough?

Perseus flew beneath the dragon's jaws. The dragon's fiery breath scorched his face, nearly blinding him, yet Perseus did not turn away. He thrust at the bare spot with all his strength. The sword plunged deep into the dragon's throat.

A fountain of blood poured from the wound. With a great moan the dragon slipped beneath the waves, never to rise again.

Perseus broke Andromeda's chains. He lifted her in his arms and flew with her through the air, all the way to her father's palace.

Cepheus and Cassiopeia wept with joy to see their daughter again. "How can we reward you?" they said to Perseus. "All the treasures of our kingdom are yours."

"I only want one treasure," Perseus told them. "Let me take Andromeda for my bride."

Andromeda and Perseus were married. Everyone in the kingdom came to the palace to celebrate their wedding. When the festivities were at their height, the door burst open. A band of young men armed with swords and spears forced their way into the hall.

"Who are you?" Perseus asked. "If you have come to join our feast, you are welcome. If you have come to cause trouble, I warn you—my sword is at my side. I am prepared to defend my bride."

"My name is Phineus," the leader said. "Andromeda is not your bride. Her father promised her to me before she was taken to the rock."

"And did you try to rescue her when she was on that rock?" Perseus asked. "No! You forgot about her, didn't you? You can forget about her now. Andromeda is my bride. I will not give her up."

"Then I will take her!" Phineus drew his sword and rushed at Perseus. His friends joined in, slashing at Perseus from all sides.

"Run, Perseus, or they will kill you!" Andromeda screamed.

"I will not run from these cowards, nor will I stain my sword with their blood," said Perseus. "I will use the power of one enemy to defeat another. All my friends, cover your eyes!" As he said this, he pulled Medusa's head from the leather bag and held it up in the faces of Phineus and his followers. They instantly turned to stone.

The wedding feast went on all night. The next morning Perseus and his bride moved into a new palace. It was built on a hilltop, with a splendid view and wonderful terraced gardens filled with trees and flowers. As well as some very unusual statues.

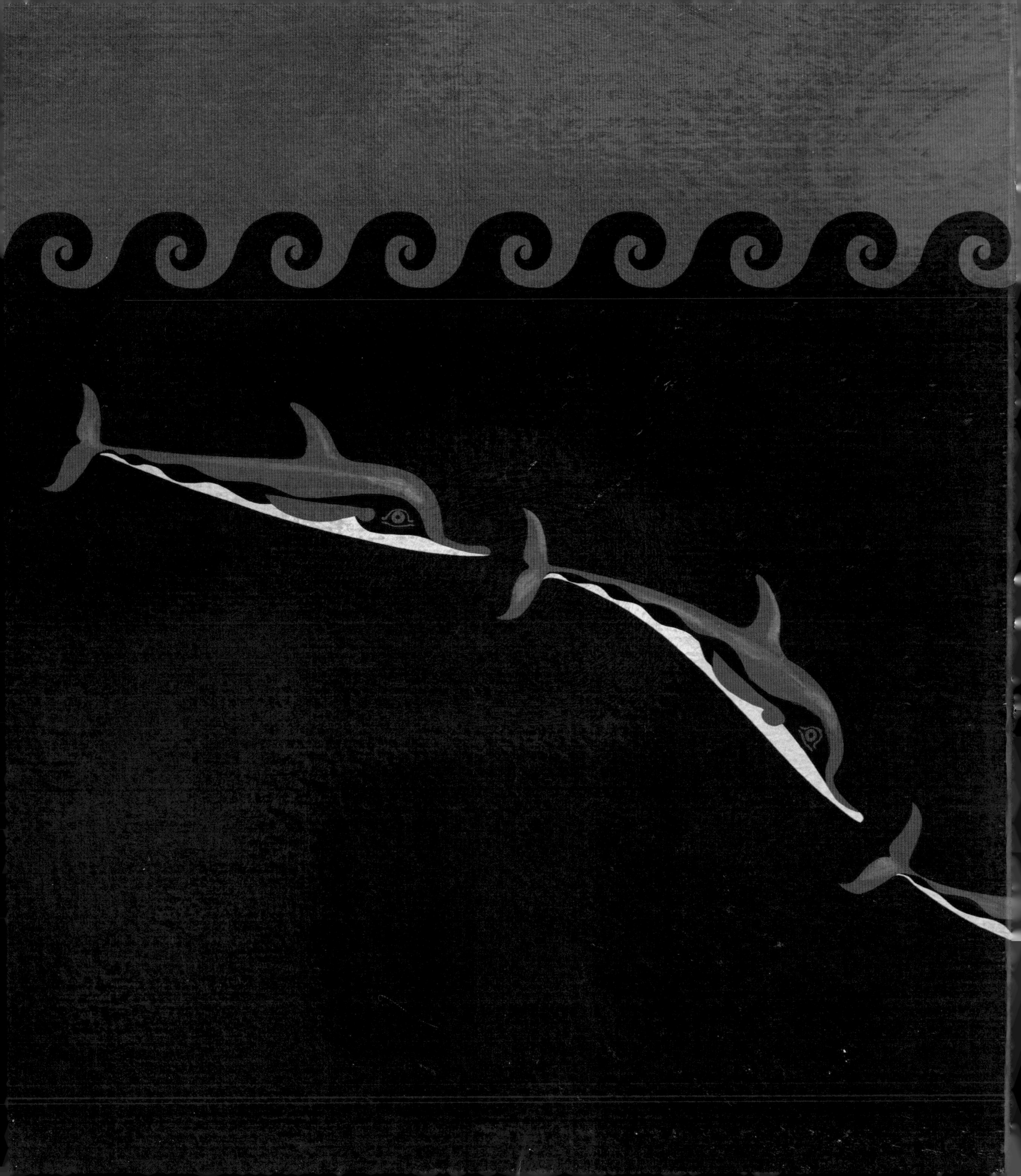